How to Outsmart a Werewolf

Eric Braun

BLACK
RABBIT
BOOKS

Hi Jinx is published by Black Rabbit Books
P.O. Box 3263, Mankato, Minnesota, 56002.
www.blackrabbitbooks.com
Copyright © 2020 Black Rabbit Books

Jen Besel, editor; Michael Sellner, designer;
Omay Ayres, photo researcher

Library of Congress Cataloging-in-Publication Data
Names: Braun, Eric, 1971- author.
Title: How to outsmart a werewolf / by Eric Braun.
Description: Mankato, Minnesota : Black Rabbit Books,
[2020] | Series: Hi Jinx. How to outsmart | Includes
bibliographical references and index.
Identifiers: LCCN 2018017045 (print) | LCCN 2018024074
(ebook) | ISBN 9781680729313 (e-book) |
ISBN 9781680729252 (library binding) | ISBN
9781644660638 (paperback)
Subjects: LCSH: Werewolves—Juvenile humor. |
Wit and humor, Juvenile.
Classification: LCC PN6231.W39 (ebook) |
LCC PN6231.W39 B73 2020 (print) |
DDC 818/.602—dc23
LC record available at
https://lccn.loc.gov/2018017045

Printed in China. 1/19

Image Credits

commons.wikimedia.org:
bignoter, 20 (both); iStock:
chavisjiam, 1 (br); ChrisGorgio,
3, 21 (face); XonkArts, 6–7
(wolf); Shutterstock: Aluna1,
15 (bkgd); Angeliki Vel, 15
(sun); Anton Brand, 16 (b);
Shutterstock, Christos Georghiou,
Cover (wolf), 2–3 (claw); 6–7 (torn
paper), 14–15 (wolf), 21 (claw),
22–23; ChromaCo, 16 (t);
Dualororua, 10 (dog); Fahmidesign,
12 (m); Freestyle_stock_photo, Cover
(bkgd), 8 (bkgd); GraphicsRF, 1, 9 (moon),
18 (jar); hchjjl, 18–19 (fleas); HitToon,
11 (ball); il67, 6 (bkgd); losw, 4 (moon);
Memo Angeles, 15 (boy), 18 (boy); NikomMaelao
Production, 15 (moon); NoPainNoGain, Cover (chemistry bkgd);
opicobello, 8-9, 10 (torn paper), 10–11 (marker stroke); Pasko Maksim,
Back Cover, 14, 23, 24 (torn paper); pitju, 5, 17, 21 (curled paper);
piyapun wannakul, 4 (wolf); Pushkin, 11 (m & r dogs); Refluo, 1 (bl),
8 (faces); Roman Samokhin, 11 (left dog); Ron Dale, 5, 9, 10, 13, 20
(marker stroke); Ron Leishman, 12 (t & b), 13; sundatoon, 1 (boy);
Teguh Mujiono, 11 (wolf); Tueris, 19 (marker stroke); your, 11 (clouds);
zooco, 18–19 (wolf) Every effort has been made to contact copyright
holders for material reproduced in this book. Any omissions will be
rectified in subsequent printings if notice is given to the publisher.

Contents

Chapter 1

Ah-oooo!

Imagine this. You're outside on a warm night. A full moon looms large in the sky. You hear howling. Suddenly you see a creature coming toward you. It stops to scratch itself with a hind leg. It sniffs the air. You're staring at a werewolf.

Pause right here. If you've ever seen a movie, you know this event could happen. You could come upon a werewolf during any full moon.

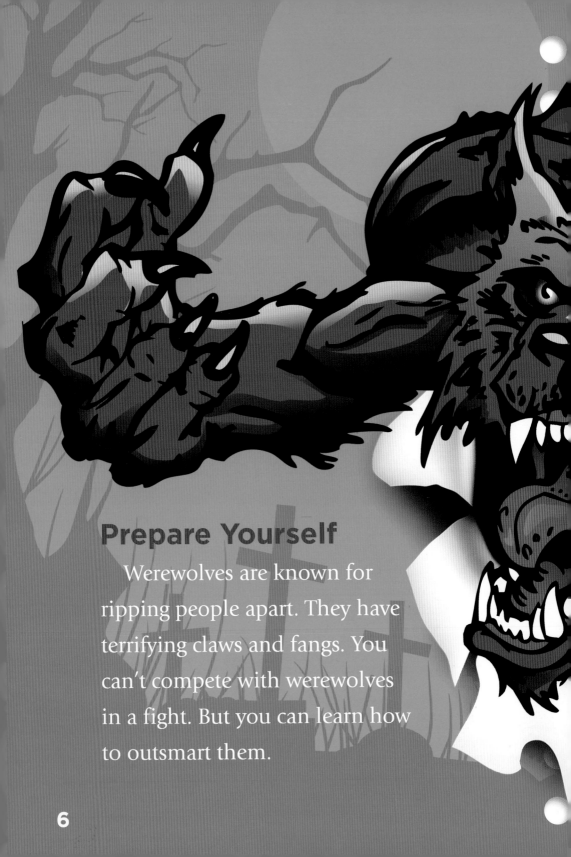

Prepare Yourself

Werewolves are known for ripping people apart. They have terrifying claws and fangs. You can't compete with werewolves in a fight. But you can learn how to outsmart them.

8

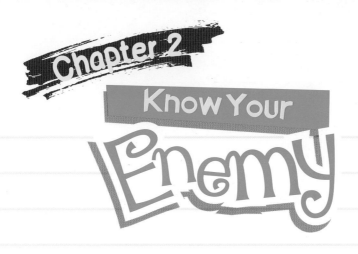

Chapter 2

Know Your Enemy

To outsmart werewolves, you have to understand them. Stories tell us that werewolves are humans who turn into wolves. Often, a full moon causes the change. The person can't control it. Being a werewolf is a terrible **curse**. For one thing, it's hard to brush all that hair.

Let's get science-y for a minute. A full moon happens every 29.5 days. The moon looks full when Earth is **aligned** between the sun and moon.

Adorable Relatives

Wolves are closely **related** to dogs. So werewolves must be too. But werewolves are not cute. They don't wiggle their butts to wag their tails. Stories say these creatures are smart, fast, and very strong.

Tip

Do not try to pet a werewolf.

Chapter 3
Outsmarting a
Werewolf

Is a werewolf ruining your neighborhood? Let's talk about ways to stop it. One tip is to stop it before it starts. Right before a full moon, find the person who is a werewolf. Tie a blindfold around their eyes. If they can't see the full moon, they can't turn into a wolf. Clever, right?

Take It for a Walk

Maybe the person already turned into a wolf. Then use its doggie **instincts**. Get a leash, and say the word "walk." The wolf will get excited. It will jump around. Put the leash on it, and take a walk. Let the wolf sniff trees. Keep walking until the sun comes up.

Bring a plastic bag in case you have to pick up wolf poop.

Play Fetch

Dogs love playing fetch. Werewolves probably do too. Hold up a tennis ball. The wolf will get excited. Pretend to throw the ball. The wolf will chase after it. It'll spend all night looking for the ball. Silly werewolf.

Scratch Attack

Another great idea is to buy a million **fleas**. (You can probably get them online.) Set them free near the werewolf. The fleas will jump right into its thick, warm coat. They will love it in there. The werewolf will scratch to get them out. You'll have time to get away.

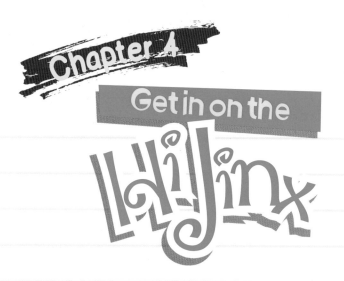

Chapter 4
Get in on the Hi Jinx

Humans can't really turn into werewolves. But it is fun to think about outsmarting one.

However, **shape-shifting** isn't all fiction. Some animals can actually change. Mutable rainfrogs can change their skin from spiny to smooth. Cuttlefish change their skins' color, pattern, and **texture**.

Maybe we should be more worried about those animals.

spiny

smooth

Take It One Step More

1. Invent a new human-animal monster. What makes it change? How does it behave?

2. Why do you think werewolf stories have been popular for so long?

3. Why do you think werewolves are evil and violent in most stories?

GLOSSARY

align (uh-LYN)—to get or fall into line

curse (KURS)—the cause of trouble or bad luck

flea (FLEE)—a wingless bloodsucking insect

instinct (IN-stingkt)—a natural, unplanned behavior in response to something

related (re-LAY-tid)—connected by a common family

shape-shift (SHAYP SHIFT)—to assume different forms

texture (TEKS-chur)—the structure, feel, and appearance of something

LEARN MORE

BOOKS

Loh-Hagan, Virginia. *Werewolves: Magic, Myth, and Mystery.* Magic, Myth, and Mystery. Ann Arbor, MI: Cherry Lake Publishing, 2017.

Peabody, Erin. *Werewolves.* Behind the Legend. New York: Little Bee Books, 2017.

Uhl, Xina M. *Werewolves.* Strange … but True? Mankato, MN: Black Rabbit Books, 2018.

WEBSITES

Are Weresolves Real (A Kids Perspective)
www.youtube.com/watch?v=OrULG556EZE

Totally Crazy Monster Myths (That Are Actually True!)
kids.nationalgeographic.com/explore/monster-myths/

Werewolf Legends
www.history.com/topics/history-of-the-werewolf-legend

INDEX